A Star From Grandma

Dedicated to my husband and our children.
I would like to thank my family and friends for their help and encouragement.

Written and Illustrated by Janet Mueller

Stella Books, Inc.
P.O. Box 4707
Edwards, CO 81632

For purchasing information please contact Stella Books, Inc. at:
Phone: (970) 926-*Star* (7827)   E-mail: info@astellabook.com

Library of Congress Control Number: 2003098406   ISBN 0-9746932-3-5

Printed in the United States of America

Michael's grandparents came to visit after his brother Gregory was born. Michael was very happy to see them.

Michael's grandmother had a present for him. It was a photo album filled with pictures of happy times Michael and his grandparents had enjoyed together.

Michael loved the present. He spent a long time sitting with his grandmother looking at the pictures and reminiscing about their adventures.

"Look Grandma," said Michael, "here we are at the zoo. See the giraffe!"

There were pictures of the times they
went swimming in the ocean,

sledding in the backyard,

Grandpa helping Michael with his first
ice-cream cone,

Michael's first birthday party and the 4th of July parade.

Michael thanked his grandmother for the present and asked if all grandmothers were so nice.

Chuckling, she replied, "I think so and I know most grandmas think their grandchildren are very special."

Then, Michael's grandmother said she had a secret gift for him and told him the following story.

Once upon a time, there was a magical grandma who had many grandchildren. Her grandchildren lived in different towns and cities throughout the world. Since the magical grandma couldn't always be with her grandchildren, she decided to give them all a gift. She thought about the gift for a long time. Finally, she decided to place a star inside every apple. The stars in the apples were secret messages to her grandchildren to remind them how very special they were. Her grandchildren enjoyed the stars so much that the magical grandma decided to share her gift. Today all grandmas can give secret stars to their special grandchildren.

After finishing the story about the secret gift, Michael's grandmother cut an apple in half and showed Michael the star.

She told Michael, "Whenever you want to be reminded how special you are, just ask your mom to cut an apple in half and you will find a little star inside from me. Remember, when you eat the apple, you will be filled with my love."

Michael asked if it would work for his baby brother, Gregory.

"Yes, it will work for all special boys and girls," replied Grandma.

Since Gregory was still a baby, they decided they would wait until Gregory was older before sharing the secret gift with him.

    That night, while playing with his dad,
Michael asked his mother if she would
please cut an apple in half for him.
    Smiling, his mom said, "Michael, you
must be a very special boy. Look at the star
Grandma left for you!"

As Michael ate the apple he thought to himself that it was the best apple he had ever tasted.